To the Halbroox Bros. From Josiah.
—J. C.

To B. F. I miss you.
—J. H.

Text copyright © 2021 Josh Crute
Illustrations copyright © 2021 Jenn Harney

First published in 2021 by Page Street Kids
an imprint of
Page Street Publishing Co.
27 Congress Street, Suite 105
Salem, MA 01970
www.pagestreetpublishing.com

Distributed by Macmillan, sales in Canada by The Canadian Manda Group

21 22 23 24 25 CCO 5 4 3 2 1

ISBN-13: 978-1-64567-284-5
ISBN-10: 1-64567-284-0

CIP data for this book is available from the Library of Congress.

This book was typeset in Basecoat.
The illustrations were created digitally.
Cover and book design by Julia Tyler for Page Street Kids

Printed and bound in Shenzhen, Guangdong, China

Page Street Publishing uses only materials from suppliers who are committed to
responsible and sustainable forest management.

Page Street Publishing protects our planet by donating to nonprofits like The Trustees,
which focuses on local land conservation.

HORNSWOGGLED!

A Wacky Words Whodunit

Josh Crute

illustrated by Jenn Harney

Deer knew something wasn't right.
He felt lighter. Uneven. Less himself.

But it wasn't until he looked in the mirror
that he discovered the awful truth. . . .

"This isn't my antler!"

"*I've been* HORNSWOGGLED!"

HORNSWOGGLE MEANS TO TRICK

So he hoofed it over to his friend, Catfish, who was doing cannonballs in the creek.

"Catfish! Catfish!
It's gone!"

"What is?"

"Can't you see?
Some cowardly critter
stole my antler!"

"Sorry," she said,
"I can't see anything
without my glasses."

But when she slipped them on, she discovered the awful truth. . . .

"These aren't my glasses!"

So they scurried over to Bison, who was kicking his feet up on the porch.

"A thief?" he said. "Let me grab my lucky boots.
We'll catch up to the rascal in no time."

But when he reached under his rocking chair,
he discovered the awful truth. . . .

"These aren't my boots!"

So they skedaddled over to the mayor, who was playing croquet with his cabinet.

"Mayor! Mayor! Some villainous varmint is stealing our stuff!"

"That's terrible!
Awful!
Offensively egregious!

Fortunately, I've penned a prizewinning speech that
will lift our spirits during these dark times."

But when he reached into his vest pocket,
he discovered the awful truth. . . .

"This isn't my speech!"

"*Attendez!* It is I, famous Belgian detective Pierre Moufette. This is not how we solve *le mystère*. We must look for clues. We must use *logique*. We must put on our thinking caps. . . ."

Then they discovered the awful truth. . . .

"Hey, that's my antler!"

words words words
BIG FINISH!
APPLAUSE!!

Fox bowed with a flourish.

"It's true!" she said. "It was I who took your things!
For I am the greatest trickster in the world.
I have **hoodwinked** emperors and **snookered** kings.
I have **bamboozled** princes and **outwitted** queens.
Why, just last week, I swapped out the crown jewels with
a bag of marbles. Let me show you!"

HOODWINK MEANS TO TRICK

SNOOKER MEANS TO TRAP

BAMBOOZLE MEANS TO CHEAT

OUTWIT MEANS TO OUTSMART

But when she reached into her fanny pack,
she discovered the awful truth. . . .

"These aren't the crown jewels!"

THE END